For Petra

A Red Fox Book

Published by Random House Children's Books
20 Vauxhall Bridge Road, London SW1V 2SA

A division of Random House UK Ltd
London Melbourne Sydney Auckland
Johannesburg and agencies throughout the world

Copyright © Ant Parker 1992

First published by Julia MacRae Books 1992

Red Fox edition 1999

10 9 8 7 6 5 4 3 2

Printed in Hong Kong

RANDOM HOUSE UK Limited Reg No. 954009

ISBN - 0-09-926564-8

Ginger

Ant Parker

RED FOX

Ginger likes
to go for a walk...

And to jump on
window sills...

And to hide
behind bushes...

And to play with
the washing...

And to sit by
the pool...

And to meet
his friends...

And to tease
the dog...

And to go home!